MY FIRST BOOK ABOUT

MASSACHUSETTS

by Carole Marsh

This activity book has material which correlates with the Massachusetts learning standards. At every opportunity, we have tried to relate information to the Massachusetts History and Social Science, English, Science, Math, Civics, Economics, and Computer Technology directives. For additional information, go to our websites: **www.massachusettsexperience.com** or **www.gallopade.com**.

GALLOPADE INTERNATIONAL

Gallopade is proud to be a member of these educational organizations and associations:

SHOPA MEMBER
School, Home, & Office Products Association

NSSEA

The Massachusetts Experience Series

My First Pocket Guide to Massachusetts!

The Big Massachusetts Reproducible Activity Book

The Massachusetts Coloring Book!

Massachusetts "Jography!": A Fun Run Through Our State

Massachusetts Jeopardy: Answers & Questions About Our State

The Massachusetts Experience! Sticker Pack

The Massachusetts Experience! Poster/Map

Discover Massachusetts CD-ROM

Massachusetts "GEO" Bingo Game

Massachusetts "HISTO" Bingo Game

A Word...
From the Author

Do you know when I think children should start learning about their very own state? When they're born! After all, even when you're a little baby, this is your state too! This is where you were born. Even if you move away, this will always be your "home state." And if you were not born here, but moved here—this is still your state as long as you live here.

We know people love their country. Most people are very patriotic. We fly the U.S. flag. We go to Fourth of July parades. But most people also love their state. Our state is like a mini-country to us. We care about its places and people and history and flowers and birds.

As a child, we learn about our little corner of the world. Our room. Our home. Our yard. Our street. Our neighborhood. Our town. Even our county.

But very soon, we realize that we are part of a group of neighbor towns that make up our great state! Our newspaper carries stories about our state. The TV news is about happenings in our state. Our state's sports teams are our favorites. We are proud of our state's main tourist attractions.

From a very young age, we are aware that we are a part of our state. This is where our parents pay taxes and vote and where we go to school. BUT, we usually do not get to study about our state until we are in school for a few years!

So, this book is an introduction to our great state. It's just for you right now. Why wait to learn about your very own state? It's an exciting place and reading about it now will give you a head start for that time when you "officially" study our state history! Enjoy,

Carole Marsh

Massachusetts
Let's Make Words!

Make as many words as you can from the letters in the words:

Massachusetts,
THE BAY STATE!

_____   _____   _____

_____   _____   _____

_____   _____   _____

_____   _____   _____

_____   _____   _____

_____   _____   _____

_____   _____   _____

_____   _____   _____

_____   _____   _____

_____   _____   _____

Massachusetts
The Sixth State

Do you know when Massachusetts became a state? Massachusetts became the sixth state on February 6, 1788.

Color Massachusetts red. Color the Atlantic and the Pacific oceans blue. Color the rest of the United States shown here green.

MA

Pacific Ocean

Atlantic Ocean

N
NW   NE
W   E
SW   SE
S

Massachusetts
State Flag

Massachusetts' current state flag was adopted in 1971. It features the state coat of arms on a field of white on both sides of the flag.

Color Massachusetts' state flag below.

Massachusetts
State Bird

Most states have a state bird. It should remind us that we need to "fly high" to achieve our goals. The Massachusetts state bird is the black-capped chickadee. Black-capped chickadees are cheerful birds. Listen for their call: "chick-adee-dee-dee."

Circle the Massachusetts state bird, then color all the birds.

The early bird gets the worm! *Yikes!*

Black–capped Chickadee

Western Meadowlark

Cardinal

Quail

Eagle

Robin

Massachusetts
State Seal and Motto

The state seal of Massachusetts is a circle with "Seal of the Republic of Massachusetts" on the edge. Inside is a blue shield with a star. A Native American holds a bow in one hand and an arrow pointing down in the other hand.

The state motto is: *Ense petit placidam sublibertate quietem.* It is written in Latin, an old language used for mottoes. It means, "By the sword we seek peace but peace only under liberty."

In 25 words or less, explain what this motto means:

_____

_____

_____

_____

Color the state seal.

...with liberty and justice for all!

Massachusetts
State Flower

Every state has a favorite flower. The state flower of Massachusetts is the mayflower. It has five small pink or white petals and a sweet smell. The mayflower likes to grow in evergreen woods or in sandy or rocky soil.

Color the pictures of the Massachusetts state flower.

Massachusetts
State Tree

The Massachusetts state tree reminds us that our roots should run deep if we want to grow straight and tall! Massachusetts' official state tree is the American elm. It is sometimes called the white elm. One tree can have over a million leaves! They grow to be 80-120 feet (24-37 meters) in height.

Finish drawing the American elm, then color it.

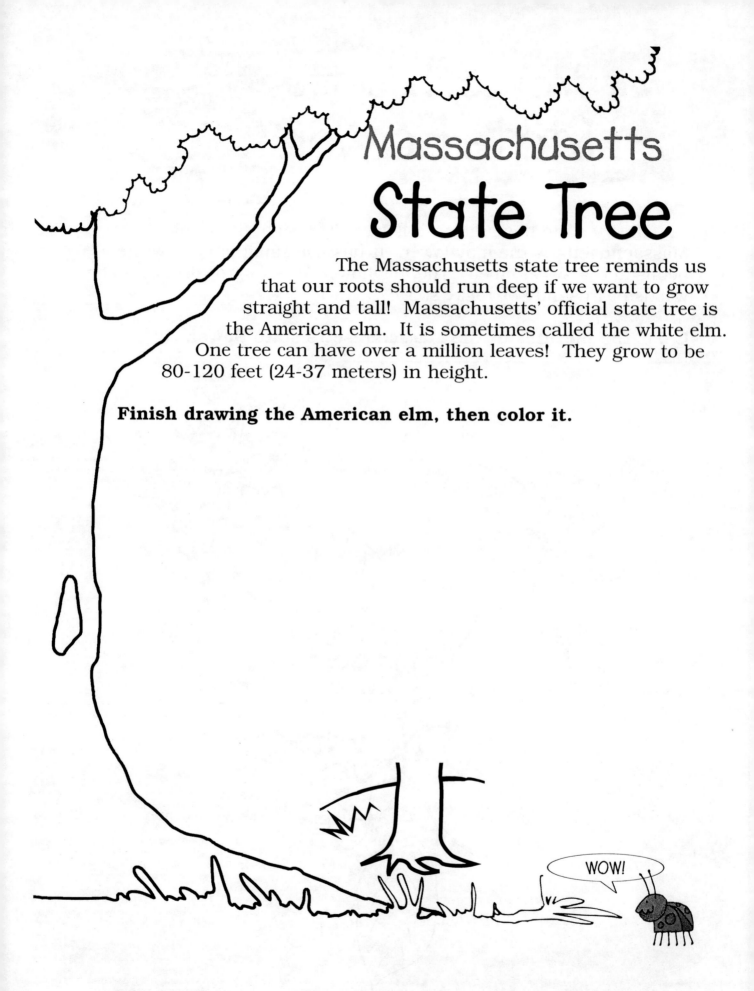

Massachusetts
State Zoo

Massachusetts is home to the Franklin Park Zoo in Boston. This zoo features an African tropical forest with gorillas.

Match the name of the zoo animal with its picture.

Zebra

Giraffe

Chimpanzee

Bear

Tiger

Massachusetts
State Explorers

In 1498, John Cabot sailed along the coast of Massachusetts. He was looking for a route to Asia. Next came Giovanni da Verrazzano. He traced the coastline. In 1605 and 1606, French explorer Samuel de Champlain charted the waters along the coast. In 1614, Captain John Smith mapped the Massachusetts Bay area. He named many of the places there.

Circle the things an explorer might have used.

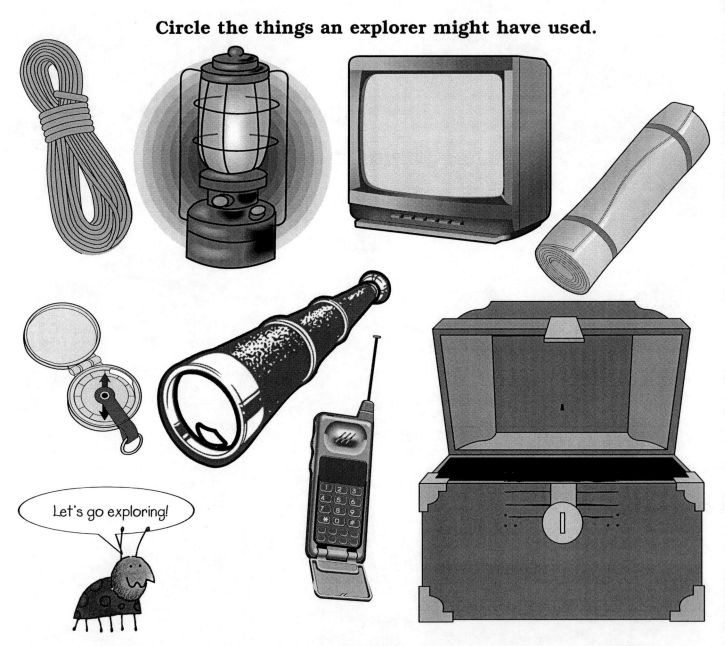

Let's go exploring!

Massachusetts
State Insect

Massachusetts' state insect is the ladybug. Ladybugs eat aphids and mites. Farmers are always glad to have them around to protect their crops from these pests. Second grade children chose the ladybug as the state insect!

Put an X by each critter that is not a ladybug and then color them all!

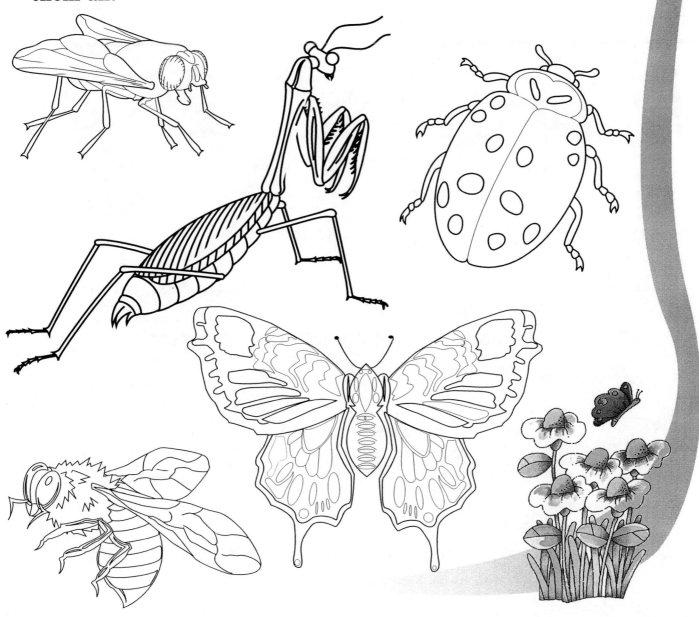

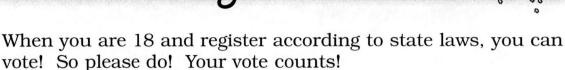

One Day I Can Vote!

When you are 18 and register according to state laws, you can vote! So please do! Your vote counts!

Your friend is running for a class office.

Here is her opponent!

She gets 41 votes!

He gets 16 votes!

ANSWER THE FOLLOWING QUESTIONS:

1. Who won?   ❑ friend   ❑ opponent

2. How many votes were cast altogether?   ⬜

3. How many votes did the winner win by?   ⬜

Massachusetts State Capital

Since 1630, Boston has been a center for government in Massachusetts. It was originally settled by British Governor John Winthrop and a group of 700 Puritans. The capitol building in Boston has a golden dome. It sits on pasture land that was owned by John Hancock.

Add your hometown to the Massachusetts map. Now add these major cities:

> **Lynn**
>
> **Worcester**
>
> **New Bedford**
>
> **Springfield**

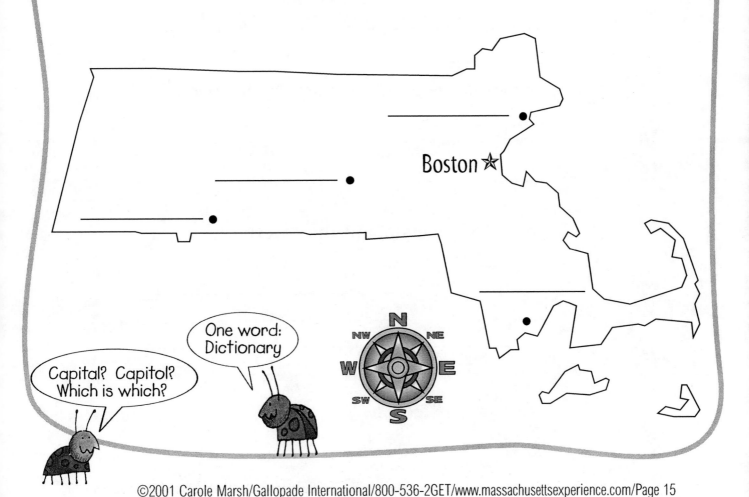

Massachusetts
Governor

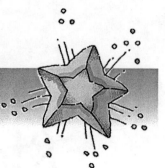

**The governor of Massachusetts is the state's leader.
Do some research to complete this biography of the governor.**

Governor's name:

_____

Paste a picture of the
governor in the box.

The governor was born in
this state:

_____

The governor has been in office since:

_____

Names of the governor's family members:

_____

_____

_____

Interesting facts about the governor:

_____

_____

_____

_____

_____

Massachusetts
Crops

Some families in Massachusetts make their living from the land. Some of the state's crops or agricultural products are:

WORD BANK

Cranberry   Potato
Beef   Sheep
Hog   Corn

UNSCRAMBLE THESE IMPORTANT STATE CROPS

ronc _____   goh _____

epesh _____   pottao _____

febe _____   bcrynaerr _____

Massachusetts
State Holidays

These are just some of the holidays that Massachusetts celebrates.

Number these holidays in order from the beginning of the year.

Columbus Day 2nd Monday in October	Thanksgiving 4th Thursday in November	Presidents' Day 3rd Monday in February
Independence Day July 4	Labor Day first Monday in September	New Year's Day January 1
Memorial Day last Monday in May	Veterans Day November 11	Christmas December 25

Massachusetts has a very special nickname. It is called the Bay State.

What other nicknames would suit Massachusetts and why?

_____

_____

_____

_____

What nicknames would suit your town or your school?

_____

_____

_____

_____

_____

What's your nickname?

Nick.

Massachusetts
How BIG is the State?

Massachusetts ranks 45th in size in the United States. It has a total area of 9,241 square miles (23,932 square kilometers).

Can you answer the following questions?

1. How many states are there in the United States?

   _____

2. This many states are smaller than Massachusetts:

   _____

3. This many states are larger than Massachusetts:

   _____

MASSACHUSETTS!

Bigfoot was here!

ANSWERS: 1-50; 2-5; 3-44

Massachusetts
People

A state is not just towns, mountains, and rivers. A state is its people! Some really important people in a state are not always famous. You may know them-they may be your mom, your dad, or your teacher. The average, everyday person is the one who makes the state a good state. How? By working hard, by paying taxes, by voting, and by helping Massachusetts children grow up to be good state citizens!

Match each Massachusetts person with his or her accomplishment.

1. John F. Kennedy

A. author of the book *Little Women*

2. John Hancock

B. first man to sign Declaration of Independence

3. Frederick Douglass

C. "father of the civil rights movement"

4. Theodore Seuss Geisel

D. author of *The Cat in the Hat*

5. Louisa May Alcott

E. 35th president of the United States

ANSWERS: 1-E; 2-B; 3-C; 4-D; 5-A

Massachusetts
Gazetteer

A gazetteer is a list of places.

Use the word bank to complete the names of some of these famous places in Massachusetts:

1.   _ _ _ _ _ _ Hill

2.   Plymouth _ _ _ _ Monument

3.   Great Point _ _ _ _ _ _ _ _ _ _

4.   Martha's _ _ _ _ _ _ _ _

5.   Old North _ _ _ _ _ _

WORD BANK

Church	Rock
Bunker	Vineyard
Lighthouse	

Massachusetts
Neighbors

No person or state lives alone. You have neighbors where you live. Sometimes they may be right next door. Other times, they may be way down the road. But you live in the same neighborhood and are interested in what goes on there.

You have neighbors at school. The children who sit in front, beside, or behind you are your neighbors. You may share books. You might borrow a pencil. They might ask you to move so they can see the board better.

We have a lot in common with our state neighbors. Some of our land is alike. We share some history. We care about our part of the country. We share borders. Some of our people go there; some of their people come here. Most of the time we get along with our state neighbors. Even when we argue or disagree, it is a good idea for both of us to work it out. After all, states are not like people—they can't move away!

Use the color key to color Massachusetts and its neighbors.

Color Key:

Massachusetts-green   New Hampshire-yellow
Vermont-blue   New York-orange
Connecticut-purple   Rhode Island-red

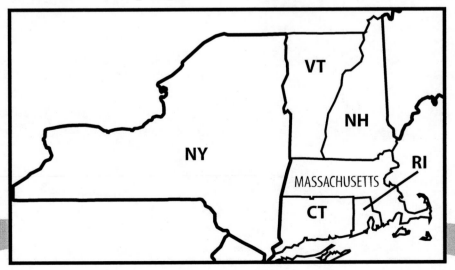

Massachusetts
Highs and Lows

Massachusetts' highest point is Mount Greylock in the Taconic Mountains. It rises 3,487 feet (1,064 meters) above sea level.

Draw a picture of a family climbing Mount Greylock.

The lowest point in Massachusetts is sea level along the Atlantic Ocean.

Draw a picture of a boating scene on the Atlantic Ocean.

Massachusetts
Old Man River

Massachusetts has many great rivers. Rivers give us water for our crops. Rivers are also water "highways." On these water highways travel crops, manufactured goods, people, and many other things—including children in tire tubes!

Here are some of Massachusetts' most important rivers:

Connecticut River

Charles River

Mystic River

Neponset River

Merrimack River

Housatonic River

Draw a kid "tubing" down the Charles River!

Massachusetts
Weather ... Or Not!

Massachusetts enjoys all four seasons and the various weather patterns they bring. The state's temperatures can drop to 25°F (-4°C) in the winter and reach 71°F (22°C) in the summer. "Nor'easters" are violent storms or hurricanes occurring along the New England coast during the late summer and fall. In winter these storms can be blizzards.

You might think adults talk about the weather a lot. But Massachusetts' weather is very important to the people of the state. Crops need water and sunshine. Weather can affect Massachusetts industries. Good weather can mean more money for the state. Bad weather can cause problems that cost money.

ACTIVITY: Do you watch the nightly news at your house? If you do, you might see the weather report. Tonight, turn on the weather report. The reporter talks about the state's regions, cities, towns, and neighboring states. Watching the weather report is a great way to learn about the state. It also helps you know what to wear to school tomorrow!

What is the weather outside now? Draw a picture.

Massachusetts
Indian Tribes

The American Indians were first on our land, long before it was a state. The Massachusetts' Indian tribes mainly included Algonquian-speaking tribes such as the: Wampanoag, Nauset, Massachuset, Nipmuc, Pocumtuc, Pennacook, and Mahican.

    Friendly Native Americans like Squanto helped Pilgrims survive their first winter by teaching them to fish and plant corn. In the fall of 1621, the first Thanksgiving was celebrated between the Pilgrims and the Native Americans.

Help Maize find her way through the maize (corn) field to her hut made of saplings!

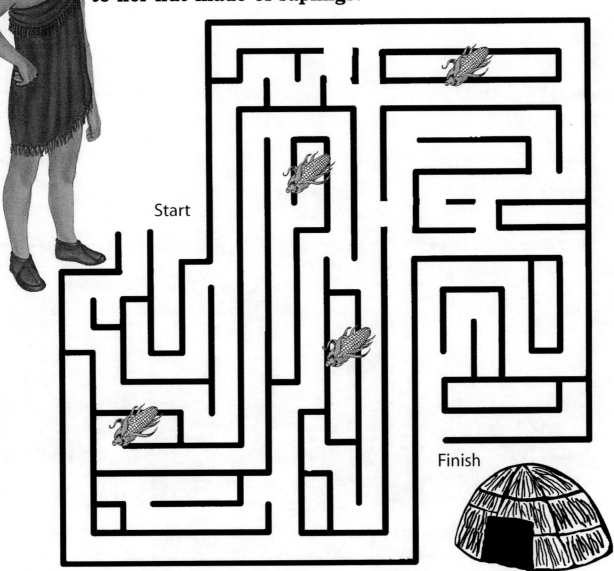

Start

Finish

Massachusetts
Website Page

Here is a website you can go to and learn more about Massachusetts:

www.netstate.com

Design your own state website page on the computer screen below.

Massachusetts
State Song

The official state song for Massachusetts is "All Hail to Massachusetts." It was adopted by the state legislature in 1966. Below is the first verse:

"All Hail to Massachusetts"
    Words and music by Arthur J. Marsh

All hail to Massachusetts, the land of the free and the brave!
For Bunker Hill and Charlestown, and flag we love to wave
For Lexington and Concord, and the shot heard round the world;
All hail to Massachusetts, we'll keep her flag unfurled.
She stands upright for freedom's light that shines from sea to sea;
All hail to Massachusetts! Our country 'tis of thee.

How does the state song make you feel? Write a verse about something in the state that means a lot to you.

_____

_____

_____

_____

_____

_____

_____

_____

Massachusetts
State Fish

The Massachusetts state fish is the Atlantic Cod. In 1784, the colonists hung a gold codfish in the Massachusetts State House to recognize the importance of this fish to their survival during early New England settlement. It is still there today! It became the state fish in 1974.

Draw six fish in the water below. Color each one a different color.

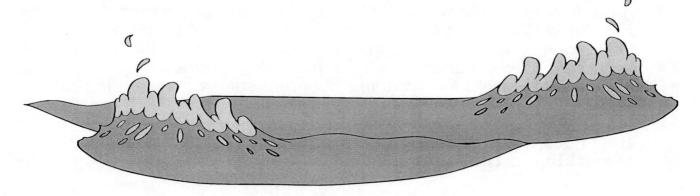

Massachusetts
Spelling Bee!

What's All The Buzz About?

Here are some words related to Massachusetts.

See if you can find them in the Word Search below.

WORD LIST

STATE	RIVER	PEOPLE	TREE	BIRD
FLAG	VOTE	FLOWER	SONG	INSECT

```
A  X  N  Y  H  N  V  S  D  G  T  R  E  P
V  O  T  E  M  A  C  S  E  A  B  A  Y  E
S  N  B  R  X  B  R  K  S  X  B  D  S  O
Y  B  P  Q  L  S  O  N  G  R  I  J  H  P
R  I  V  E  R  P  P  L  R  T  Y  U  E  L
Q  R  E  R  R  Y  Z  E  E  R  T  O  N  E
R  D  P  P  A  E  A  O  N  E  C  K  A  R
S  X  O  C  E  A  W  C  T  C  E  S  N  I
P  O  B  U  Y  U  Y  O  E  O  L  L  D  O
Q  U  F  L  A  G  R  K  L  L  X  Z  O  P
Z  X  R  D  G  H  R  E  U  F  L  L  A  L
M  R  D  W  Q  N  M  N  S  T  A  T  E  Z
```

Massachusetts
Trivia

- Fenway Park is the smallest major league baseball park in the United States.
- The Boston Celtics have been named one of the best sports franchises of all time.
- The textile industry was the most important industry in Massachusetts for about 100 years during the 19th and early 20th centuries.
- Boston is part of a megalopolis that runs throughout northeastern Massachusetts.
- Bay Staters sometimes call Boston "the Hub."
- Thousands of tourists come to Cape Cod each year. Sandwich is the oldest town on the cape.
- Whale-watching cruises are a very popular attraction.
- The Wampanoag people taught the early colonists how to make pemmican out of venison and cranberries.
- Granary Burying Ground has the graves of famous leaders like Samuel Adams.
- Freedom Trail is a walking tour in downtown Boston. It points out the major landmarks of the city during Colonial and Revolutionary times.
- Crispus Attucks, an African-American patriot, was one of the first men killed during the Boston Massacre.

Now add a fact you know about Massachusetts here:

_____

_____

_____

_____